I Went to the Farm

For my grandchildren, Hannah and Ben — R.M.

For my Kimmie — P.-H.G.

Text © 2000 Ruth Miller
Illustrations © 2000 Per-Henrik Gürth

Kids Can Press acknowledges the financial support of the Ontario Arts Council, the Canada Council for the Arts and the Government of Canada, through the BPIDP, for our publishing activity.

Published in Canada by
Kids Can Press Ltd.
29 Birch Avenue
Toronto, ON M4V 1E2

Published in the U.S. by
Kids Can Press Ltd.
2250 Military Road
Tonawanda, NY 14150

www.kidscanpress.com

The artwork in this book was rendered in watercolor.
The text is set in Stone Sans.

Edited by Debbie Rogosin
Designed by Julia Naimska and Marie Bartholomew
Printed and bound in Hong Kong by Book Art Inc., Toronto

The hardcover edition of this book is smyth sewn casebound.
The paperback edition of this book is limp sewn with a drawn-on cover.

CM 00 0 9 8 7 6 5 4 3 2 1
CM PA 02 0 9 8 7 6 5 4 3 2 1

National Library of Canada Cataloguing in Publication Data

Miller, Ruth, 1937–
    I went to the farm

ISBN 1-55074-705-3 (bound)   ISBN 1-55074-709-6 (pbk.)

I. Gürth, Per-Henrik II. Title.

PS8576.I5558I293 2000   jC813'.54   C00-930012-0
PZ7.M44Iw 2000

Kids Can Press is a Nelvana company

I Went to the Farm

written by **Ruth Miller**

illustrated by **Per-Henrik Gürth**

Kids Can Press

I went to the farm one summer day,

To see if the animals wanted to play.

The cow said, "Moo," and ate some hay.
The horse just whinnied and walked away.

The sheep and the goat were resting there.
They blinked and yawned and sniffed the air.

The turkey and geese and chickens, too,
All had other things to do.

The donkey brayed and shook his head.
He seemed to want to nap instead.

The swans and the ducks went paddling by.
They didn't stop when I said, "Hi!"

The pig and her piglets slept in their pen.
"Would you like to play?" I asked, and then ...

Beside the barn and under a tree,
I spied a little kid like me.

With smiling face and twinkly eyes,
Just my age and just my size.

And I could tell — oh lucky day!
I'd found someone who wanted to play!

The animals watched as we tumbled about.

"That looks like fun!" I heard them shout.

The cow said, "Moo, may I play with you?"
And she danced a jig and the horse danced, too.

The chickens clucked and the ducks said, "Quack,"
And they buried themselves in the big haystack.

The nanny goat played catch with the sheep,
Who caught the ball with a flying leap,

While the donkey and geese played hide-and-seek,
And the turkey tickled the pig with its beak.

"Would you like a ride in my boat?" said a swan.
"Oh, yes!" we said, and we both climbed on.

We floated left and we paddled right.
We laughed and giggled and held on tight.

We played and played until day's end,
The animals, I and my new-found friend.

Then we waved good-bye and we skipped away.
"We'll come back again when you want to play!"

And I'm certain I heard the animals say ...
"Haven't we had a most wonderful day!"